WEDDING TIME
Copyright © 2017 C. Kaye
All rights reserved.
Published by C. Kaye Books

eBook ISBN: 978-0-9982167-2-0
Print ISBN: 978-0-9982167-3-7

Printed in the USA.

Cover Design and Interior Format

Wedding
TIME

A Novella

C. KAYE

OUR TIME FOR LOVE #1.5

To my daughters, Amber & Lindsey.
Being your mom is the greatest thing ever.

"Love recognizes no barriers.
It jumps hurdles, leaps fences,
penetrates walls to arrive at its
destination full of hope."

– Maya Angelou

Chapter 1

GEMMA

THE REFLECTION IN THE MIRROR brings tears to my eyes. I turn slowly. It is a simple floor length dress of ivory satin and lace with a very short train. No frills or fluff. Just simple beauty.

"This is it." I continue to turn. "This is the one."

"It's perfect, Gemma! It's like it was made just for you." Kathleen reaches out to hug me.

"It really is made for you. It's so beautiful." Tiba joins Kathleen. The three of us stand in front of the mirror with our arms wrapped around each other, our eyes glistening with tears.

Sometimes I still can't believe I will soon marry Raef Alvero. Just a few short months ago, I thought I would never see him again. Then he came barreling back into my life. It was a rocky road at the beginning, but we survived and came out stronger on the other side. Raef, Charley, and I are now a family. A family that is planning a small wedding to make it all official.

We separate and Tiba takes my hand to twirl me again and again. As I watch my reflection in the mirror, my tears turn to laughter. I throw my head back as I spin and enjoy the moment. Kathleen giggles with her hand over her mouth and Tiba laughs with me.

"Raef is going to be blown away when he sees you in this," Tiba says.

"I hope he loves it as much as I do."

"Oh, Gemma. He's going to love it even more than you do. You look beautiful." Kathleen beams at me. "Let's get you changed so we can buy it. I can't believe it doesn't even need any alterations. It is truly meant for you."

We move back to the dressing area. Kathleen and Tiba help me out of the dress and get it back in the protective covering. I can't help but run my fingers over the lace before I zip up the bag. Kathleen takes it to the counter to hold as I lead Tiba, my maid-of-honor, to the front of the store.

"Now, time to find you something, Tiba. It has to be pink. I let Charley pick her own dress and, of course, pink is the color she chose."

We go through rack after rack of elegant gowns. After almost an hour, Tiba finds a lovely one. Her caramel skin is highlighted by the soft pink color. The short, one-shoulder, chiffon style flatters her figure.

"Wow, Tiba. You look amazing." I am almost as excited for her dress as I am for mine.

"I do love this one." Tiba holds the loose material in each hand and slowly turns in front of the mirror. "Are you sure it fits with the style of your wedding?"

"You know my wedding doesn't have a theme—well, other than pink. It's just me, you and Charley on my side. I want you to be comfortable. And you do look beautiful in that dress. If you love it, then I say let's get it." I squeeze Tiba's hand and smile at my best friend. Tiba is the sister I never had. I can't imagine getting married without her by my side.

"Okay, then. Let's get it!" Tiba claps her hands in excitement. She glances in the mirror one last time and heads to the dressing room.

Once we have everything at the check-out counter, Tiba and I both pull out our payment cards from our purses.

Before we can pay, Kathleen bats at our hands. "Put those away, girls. The dresses are my treat." Tiba's mouth drops open in confusion.

"Oh, Kathleen," I gasp. "You can't do this! It's way too much. You're already letting us have the wedding at the farm. I can't let you do this."

Kathleen places her hands on my shoulders. "We may not share blood but you're a daughter to me. Let me do this for you. Let me give you the wedding of your dreams."

Tears of joy stream down my face. Since the death of my parents in a tragic car accident when I was 18, Kathleen and Jack have become my surrogate parents. To know Kathleen feels so deeply about this makes me love her even more. I know if I turn down her offer, I will deeply offend her.

"Thank you, Kathleen." I throw my arms around her in a tight embrace.

"It's settled then. I've got this. You girls decide where we are doing lunch while I finish this up." And just like that, Kathleen gets down to the business of purchasing both dresses. I pull Tiba aside.

"Oh my, Gemma! Did she really just by our dresses?" Tiba exclaims.

"Yes. Yes, she did. I feel guilty about it, but it seems to mean a lot to her. I guess we just have to accept that she wants to do this for us." I sigh, thinking about Kathleen and my own mother. Sadness creeps into my heart. I wish Mom was here with me. "She's the only mother I have now."

"She definitely takes the job seriously. I'm still in shock! You're so lucky to have her." Tiba's voice breaks at the end. She hasn't had a relationship with her parents in many years. Her statement reminds me of just how lucky I really am.

"I'm sorry, Tiba. I didn't even think of how you might be feeling."

"No worries, girlie. I've been alone for so long, I really don't know any other way to be. And don't think I begrudge you for having them. I love that for you. They've been good to me, too. Always inviting me for Sunday dinner. And now this. Kathleen could've easily bought your dress and not mine. She's an angel." Tiba smiles. "So, enough of the feels. Where are we eating lunch? Shopping makes me hungry!"

We both laugh and toss out names of various restaurants. By the time we finally decide on a place, Kathleen is finished with the purchase. We gather our dresses and set out for lunch.

The next two hours are spent with great food and even better conversation. We discuss the wedding, making decisions on flowers and decorations.

We move on to discussions of Charley. She is always a favorite topic when spending time with Kathleen. I keep them both laughing with stories about Charley and Raef and how she rules the roost in our house. That little girl keeps him on his toes and makes for great conversation.

After lunch, we go shoe shopping. The rest of the afternoon is spent buying shoes, not only for the wedding but just for fun. Being a single parent for so many years, shoe purchases were few and far between. Recently, Raef made me promise to treat myself more often. I had avoided accepting money from him but he insisted that since we were getting married, I needed my own credit card. I may make him proud today with my purchases.

"Wow! I've never spent that much on myself in my life. Do I really need this many pairs of shoes?" I feel a little guilty about my excessive purchases.

"Of course you do," Tiba exclaims. "Shoes are a woman's guilty pleasure."

"She's right, Gemma," Kathleen chimes in. "We need our treats. Plus, your lifestyle is different now. You can splurge sometimes."

"Well, at least I got some new shoes for Charley." I attempt to justify how much I just charged to Raef's card.

"Your little diva will be so excited. I can just picture her modeling all of them for Raef. He'll be as excited as she is." Kathleen can't help but chuckle. She knows how Charley has Raef wrapped around her finger. I snicker at that image myself.

The three of us pile into my car and drive back to Granier. After a long day spent in the city, I am ready for the quietness of my little town. Fortunately, we beat the major traffic and make the trip in the normal hour. We transfer Tiba and Kathleen's purchases to their cars and after goodbyes and another heartfelt thank you to Kathleen, I move my bags into our apartment before retrieving Charley from her babysitter. This was a very special day in so many ways. My heart swells from the wonderful friends I have in Kathleen and Tiba.

Chapter 2

RAEF

THE TIME ON MY OFFICE clock catches my eye. I shut down my computer and lean back in my chair. Since the fallout from my father trying to keep me from Gemma by kidnapping our daughter, I have been swamped with work. Alvero & Alvero's public image took quite a hit with the negative publicity from the incident. Thankfully our swift response highlighted my father being removed from the company. We have mitigated the damage to a certain extent, but it seems to be a daily struggle to build back the public following we once had. Even with the excessive workload, I am determined to keep my new family first. That means no long hours at the office.

On my way out the door, I stop by my assistant's desk. When I returned to the company in my father's position, I moved Ashley with me. Dad's assistant was traumatized by what he had done and decided not to stay on with the company. I made sure she had a good severance package and helped her transition to a position with another company.

"Time to head home, Ashley."

"I'll head out shortly. I need to finish typing this report so you can have it for your board meeting in the morning. The phone has been crazy this afternoon so I'm a little behind." Ashley tilts her head toward her computer screen. I *do* need the report finished but I hate seeing her stay when I am leaving.

"I'll hang around until you finish. I thought the calls would lessen with time. Doesn't seem to be happening though." Ashley has fielded calls from reporters for weeks. I'm waiting for something else to happen in the city to take the spotlight away from us, but that hasn't happened yet. The media seems determined to keep the story alive.

"No, Raef. You head home. You have a long drive. I just have to hop across town." Ashley smiles. "I like this new you. Family looks good on you."

"Those two are the most important things to me now," I say in regards to Gemma and Charlotte. "This place is important, but they are my world. Don't stay too long. You can always finish in the morning."

"I won't. Bye, Raef." Ashley turns back to her computer and resumes typing.

"Bye, Ash." I head out of the office to the elevator.

I shoot off a quick text to Gemma on my way to the car.

About to head home. Hope traffic isn't too bad. Can't wait to see you.

She responds immediately. *Be careful. Can't wait to see you too!*

Gemma has been shopping. I can't wait to find out if she found a dress. Just spending time with Kathleen and Tiba should have made for a good day for her. The three have worked on the wedding fervently. I've been the good fiancé and only given my opinion on choices when asked. Of course, our little one chose the wedding colors from day one. Pink. Everything has to be pink. We are raising a diva princess.

Since Gemma and I reunited, I have wanted to make

her my wife. Each hour that passes brings us closer to our nuptials, but it still seems a lifetime away. I carry the ring I will place on her finger in my pocket every day. It's a reminder of the vows we will soon share.

Thoughts of the wedding remind me that we don't have a confirmed officiant. Neither of us has attended a church in years, so we decided to find someone close to us that would be willing to become qualified to legally perform the ceremony. My first thought had been my brother, Daniel, but he will stand with me as my best man. Since Jack Greenwood is the only father figure either of us have and he will escort Gemma, he is not an option, either.

My next thought had turned to my best friend. Moss and I have remained close even though he long ago moved to Chicago. He is a very well-known attorney, but he made his fortune early in life through investments. He is a shark when it comes to Wall Street and could walk away from practicing law completely. Instead, his firm takes cases to represent those who can't afford high-profile attorneys, but are in desperate need of someone to help them prove their innocence. He has also created a home for victims of sex-trafficking so they have a place to recover and pre-pare to re-enter society. When I told Gemma of all the things Moss works so hard to accomplish for people, she immediately agreed he was the one to marry us. Moss was thrilled when I asked him.

I call him on my drive home to see if he has obtained his credentials. Surprisingly, he answers on the first ring.

"Well, hello there," Moss greets me. "Backed out on the wedding and calling to tell me?" Moss chuckles. He knows what Gemma means to me.

"Never and you know it." I laugh back to him. "Just checking to see if we have an officiant."

"Good news. You do. My internet-issued official license

is ready to go."

"Perfect! When will you fly in?" I ask.

"The day before the wedding. Are we going out for one last blast for a bachelor party?" Moss asks the same question Daniel recently asked me. I have no interest in going out and partying with the guys. I would rather be with Gemma and Charlotte. Gemma and I discussed it and agreed we would go out for a few hours with our friends together instead of separately.

"Not a chance, man. I already feel like my bachelor days are well behind me. Gemma and I are going to a bar in Granier with a few of our friends that evening. We would love for you to join us." Moss hasn't been back home in about a year. This will be a great chance to spend time with him to catch up on things.

"Acting like an old married man already." Moss chuckles. "I'll be there. Text me the address and time. My flight arrives around noon so that will give me a little time run by my loft." Moss maintains a residence in the city for when he visits. His main home may be Chicago but he still has New Orleans in his blood.

Moss and I chat for a few more minutes. He tells me about his latest case and I tell him stories about Charlotte. He rags me more about being so settled while I encourage him to consider it as an option for himself. Of course, he gives me his standard answer. "I will never tie myself to one woman when there are so many out there." That seems like a good place to end the conversation so we say our goodbyes and end the call.

Before I know it, I'm home. Home has become Gemma's little apartment. We are crammed wall-to-wall in the apartment but none of us mind. Gemma has no idea I plan to buy a house here in Granier for her wedding present. I had given her the five hair salons when my father tried to close the one where she worked. They were going to be a wedding gift for her until my father forced my hand with his attempts to keep us apart. I wound up giving them to her then, before I proposed. Her job security at the time was more important than holding the salons as a gift. It all worked out because a house will be a total surprise for her.

I have had a realtor looking for the perfect home and today she let me know she may have found it. I have Max meeting us at the house first thing tomorrow morning. He is the only one I trust to make sure the house is safe for my girls. His work as a contractor gives him the knowledge I don't have, and his relationship with Gemma and Charley means he will be honest with me about the structure. I just hope he doesn't slip up and tell Gemma. I don't want him to wind up ruining my wedding gift surprise.

Max still seems wary around me. He doesn't want to trust me with Gemma but he can't deny how I feel. He sees it whenever he is around the two of us. No one can miss my love for Gemma. There is a silly smile of pure happiness plastered on my face any time we are together and I am constantly touching her. I can't keep my hands from her. I shower her with affection and gifts, but none of that will ever equal the treasures she has given me— her love and our daughter. I am the luckiest man in the world to be able to have her in my life. Even luckier to have Charlotte. Just a few short months ago my life was so different, focused only on work. Now I live for my family and work is secondary.

Ready to see my girls, I hop out of my vehicle. I chuckle to myself on the short walk to the apartment. I can only imagine what stories Charlotte has for me today. I love hearing her tell me about her day and each night together is special. Then when she goes to bed, it's just me and Gemma. Nothing could be sweeter. Time with my two girls is the perfect end to a day.

Chapter 3

GEMMA

THE FRONT DOOR OPENS AND I don't have to wonder who it is. Charley's voice carries through the small space. "Hey, Daddy!" Raef's low chuckle reaches me and I can picture him pick her up for a hug. I smile at how close the two have become.

At first, I wondered if I would be jealous of their relationship. It had been just the two of us for so long. But as I see their connection grow—reading stories, cuddling on the couch while watching movies, playing with her dolls–I am thrilled with how close they have become. I never imagined how much having a father would mean to Charley. She has absolutely blossomed with Raef in her life.

I wipe my hands on the kitchen towel and head into the living room. Raef's gaze seeks me out before I am even through the door. It's like he can sense when I am coming. Well, he *can* sense *that*. I laugh to myself. Dirty thoughts aside, we have an intense connection. My body tingles whenever he is near. I smile broadly at the sight before me. Raef is barely in the front door, but Charley's little arms are wrapped tightly around his neck as he holds her.

There is a heat in Raef's blue eyes and his slow pace toward me is almost predatory. I meet him in the middle of the room and he pulls me into the side of his body with his free arm. Charley continues chattering and he turns his head to the side to greet me with a kiss. The kiss is short. Charley puts her hand on his cheek and pulls it back toward her.

"Ugh, Daddy!" Charley crinkles her nose in exasperation. "Stop kissing Mommy and listen to me!" Raef winks at me before returning his attention to her.

"Sorry, little one. I had to tell your Mommy hello, too. Continue with your story." Charley rattles on as I point to the kitchen. Raef takes the hint and we all gather around the table. I prepared a simple meal tonight since I was in the city all day.

It still seems so strange that this has become his home. I told Raef early on that Charlotte and I would move to the city with him since he worked there, but he wouldn't have it. He said Granier would be our home and it has been. He enjoys the calm atmosphere our town provides over the craziness of the city.

Charley talks through the meal except when she is actually eating her sub sandwich. She tries to talk then, but I remind her about her manners. We hear every detail about her day at the sitter's apartment. Every detail. Raef never seems frustrated when Charley talks. He listens to everything she says and interacts with her during the conversation. That is, when she stops long enough for someone else to speak. Tonight is like most nights with Raef and I spending most of our conversation with Charley as opposed to each other. Our time comes later in the evening.

Raef gives me a quick peck on the cheek as I go to take Charley for her bath. He stays in the kitchen to clean up.

This has become our nightly routine. I am amazed that a man of Raef's professional stature wants to help around the house. He tells me all the time that it's his way to make sure he is involved in all parts of our family since I did it alone for so many years. Being involved is very important to Raef. He has been hands-on since he moved in with us.

After bath time, our routine consists of either a board game or some other activity Charley plans for us. This is our family time and a four-year-old rules it. Tonight we play with the doctor set Raef brought home recently. Charley is the doctor and we are the patients. She has put us in the hospital and is currently checking Raef's heartbeat. She "doctors" us until bedtime.

While Raef puts Charley to bed, I slip into our room. While wedding shopping, we made a quick stop in a lingerie store where I bought a negligée for our wedding night. I decided to buy another one for tonight. It is lavender lace and satin, and leaves little to the imagination. Raef won't expect my surprise.

All the bags from the shopping trip are scattered around our bedroom. But not my wedding dress. I sent it to the farm with Kathleen so I wouldn't break down and show it to Raef. I dig through the bags I haven't had a chance to unpack yet and find the negligée. It doesn't take me long to change into the sexy garment and cover it with a robe. Just as I finish, Raef opens the door.

"Whew, what a day." Raef pulls me to him and kisses me. "I'm glad Charlotte fell asleep quickly tonight. Only one book."

"Alexis took the kids to the park this afternoon. Lucky for you, she was worn out. It didn't stop her from talking all night though." I shake my head when I think of how much that child can prattle.

"I keep telling you, she's just like my sister. Marie is a grown woman and still chatters all the time. You'll see when you meet her." Raef glances around the room at the bags. "Looks like you had a productive shopping trip today."

"We did. Very much so." Guilt gnaws me. "I may have spent a little too much."

"It's fine. I want you to have the things you want. I want to spoil you." Raef kisses me again. "The big question is, did you find a wedding dress?"

"I did. Oh, Raef, it's so beautiful! It's like it was made for me. It just felt right when I put it on. Kathleen and Tiba thought it was perfect."

"I can't wait to see you in it, but you could wear a potato sack. Just as long as you marry me." Raef kisses me a little harder and longer this time.

"I'm not going to wear a potato sack and you have to wait to see the dress. I do have a surprise for you that you can have now." I back away from him with a devilish grin on my face.

"Gemma, you don't have to buy me things. I just need you and Charlotte."

"I think you might change your mind once you see this." I slowly untie the belt to my robe. "But then again, if you don't want it, I can return it." I let the robe slide off my shoulders. Raef's blue eyes widen, darkening with desire. He opens his mouth to speak but no words come out.

"I guess I need to change if I'm going to return this." I play coy, tucking my head and gazing at Raef through my lashes. He growls as he steps to me and pulls me in tightly against his body. His erection presses against me.

"No way in hell that is going back." Kisses trail across my neck. I tilt my head to give him better access. I shiver as his lips connect with my skin.

"So, do you like it?" I ask breathlessly. Raef grabs my hips and grinds me against him.

"Best surprise ever," he whispers against my neck. He stops suddenly and with his finger under my chin, gently turns me to look into his eyes. "Other than Charlotte, that is." I smile at the genuineness in his words. I kiss him quickly and nudge him to the edge of the bed.

"Well, Mr. Alvero, since you like your gift, I think you should let me undress you." I start with his tie. He always loosens it when he gets home, but he leaves it so I can take it off. There is something so sexy about removing a man's tie. I make quick work of the tie and unbutton his shirt.

"Soon-to-be Mrs. Alvero, I think you are absolutely correct. Remove away." Raef's tries to help me with his belt.

I slap at his hand. "This is my show."

Raef laughs but stops trying to help. I remove each piece of clothing, taking the time to fold each and place it on the dresser.

"Woman, you are killing me." Raef moans. "Let me take off the rest of my clothes," he practically begs.

"Nope. My surprise, my time. And I want to take it slow." I continue with my work. It doesn't take me long to have him completely naked in front of me.

I give Raef a small push. "Lay down, Mr. Alvero. I want to have my way with you tonight."

Raef falls to the bed and slides back. His long body sprawls completely across the bed. He crooks his finger for me to join him.

"My surprise, my time, remember?" I crawl onto the bed with him but I don't maneuver beside him like he expects. Instead, I stay at the foot of the bed. As I run by hands up his legs, his eyes shine with pleasure and passion.

He knows my plans. I lick my lips in anticipation. Being in control of Raef's pleasure is quite empowering.

"Your surprise, your time," Raef repeats as I trail kisses along his thighs, moving from one to the other. His tosses his head back and his hands grip the bed covers. I inch toward his impressive length as he seems to get even harder.

Raef squirms as I continue light kisses on his thighs. I lightly run my hand over his length and he practically jumps off the bed. With his eyes closed, he never saw it coming. I chuckle against his thigh and my hand wraps around him.

"God, Gemma! You really are killing me now!" Raef squirms more in an attempt to get me where he wants me. I decide to put him out of his misery and wrap my lips around him.

"*Yessss!*" Raef hisses between his teeth.

I leisurely take him in and out of my mouth as his grips the back of my head. His hips find a life of their own and I pick up my speed, working him with both my hand and mouth. It doesn't take long before Raef grows even more. I know he is close. He taps my head to warn me, even though he knows I won't move.

Raef lets go with a groan. "I love you, Gemma! I love you so damned much!"

Raef pulls me up beside him. I kiss him as I snuggle into his body.

"I love you, too, Raef," I whisper against his chest.

Chapter 4

RAEF

MY THOUGHTS ALL MORNING HAVE been on the *surprise* Gemma gave me last night. She never ceases to amaze me. Just when I think I know what to expect from her, she does something so out of character. I must admit, I loved every minute of it. I also loved how her cheeks turned that delicious shade of pink this morning when I thanked her again for my surprise. I smile at the thought.

I bring my thoughts back to the present as I pull into the drive of the house I may purchase. The first thing I see is the sprawling porch across the front. I picture Gemma in a swing reading one of those romance books she loves so much. The light gray color with white and black trim makes it very stately. It's a simple color scheme that works well with the expansive landscaping.

I notice Max is here but the realtor has not yet made it. I park and walk to the porch where Max waits. He wears his ever-present scowl. He really needs to lighten up and find something that makes him happy.

"Thanks for meeting me here this morning, Max." I extend my hand. Reluctantly he takes it for a handshake.

"I'm here for Gemma and Charlotte. If you are buying

this house, I will look at it for them." His scowl deepens. I blow him off. I'm not in the mood for a confrontation. Plus, I promised Gemma I would try to get along with this guy, even though I'm still not comfortable around him.

"What do you think of the house so far?" I ask to move the subject along.

"I walked around the outside. It looks to be well-built. It can't be very old based on some of the materials used." Max waves his hand around toward the house like I should know what materials he refers to. I don't, but nod in agreement.

"I like that it isn't on the main road. This neighborhood provides more privacy than most. I think Gemma will like that." I try to make conversation to fill the time. I sigh with relief when the realtor arrives. "We can see the inside now."

After quick introductions between Max and my agent, Stella, we enter the house. The first thing I notice is the staircase. It's a grand feature in the house with a combination of wooden steps and detailed iron railing. I love that it isn't directly in front of the door but is placed slightly off to the right. And it curves as it rises. It makes quite a statement. We move throughout the lower level before heading upstairs. The farther we move through the house the more in love I fall. The hardwood floors are pristine and the finishes are all top of the line. Gemma will love this place.

The bottom floor has an open floor plan, and the top floor is filled with four bedrooms and four bathrooms. Plenty of room for us to grow our family. Once done inside, we head to the back yard. There I am greeted with a big surprise. Not only is there a beautiful swimming pool, but also an outdoor kitchen area with a fireplace.

This will be the perfect place for us to entertain. I look around at the yard. It is very large and completely fenced in with a tall white privacy fence. The realtor points out that the property extends into the woods behind the fence. That is an added bonus I didn't expect and helps ensure our privacy.

Max wanders outside to join us. We had lost him in the house earlier. He went his own way checking various things while I meandered through the house. I look to him expectantly, anxious to hear what he has to say. He nods my way before he speaks.

"I'm not a home inspector but as a contractor, I can tell you this house was well built. I made a few calls and found out the name of the builder. I can vouch that he is good at what he does. He hires quality employees and makes sure the work is done correctly. I think it will be a good investment." I let out a breath as Max finishes. I had hoped he wouldn't find anything wrong with the house. I can already picture our family here and didn't want to find something that would prevent me from buying it.

"Thank you, Max." I turn back to the realtor. "Stella, I want to put in a full cash offer today. Since the homeowners have already moved, I want to close this deal as soon as possible."

"I will take care of it, Mr. Alvero. Expect to hear from me this afternoon. The homeowners are motivated to sell so they should be pleased with your offer." Stella and I shake hands and she quickly heads to her car.

"Thank you again, Max." I extend my hand to him again. "You were the only person I trusted to help me with this." Max looks at my extended hand, his hesitation is evident. His actions today have left me with concerns regarding Max's feelings. Does he possibly still have feelings for Gemma that make him so stand-offish to me?

Gemma assures me he doesn't, but I am beginning to realize that she may be missing something.

"Like I said, I did it for Gemma and Charley." Max gets in his truck and leaves without any further words.

I watch Max drive down the road. Gemma may be fooling herself if she thinks Max and I will ever be friends. I sigh and turn back to the house, taking it all in one more time. This is going to be home for us. I can't wait to show it to Gemma and Charlotte. I look at my watch to see more time has passed than I realized. I need to get back to the city for this morning's board meeting.

I don't make it far out of town before my phone rings. When I see it is my mother, I quickly answer the call.

"Hey, Mom. What's up?" I ask.

"Raeford." Mom shutters in a breath. "I just received a call." She pauses again.

"What is it, Mom?" Worry settles in the pit of my stomach. From the shaky sound of my mother's voice, I know something is terribly wrong.

"He's dead. Your father's dead." The sound of my mother crying fills the car.

"What do you mean *he's dead*? What happened?" I'm confused, not comprehending the news.

"Your father was in the cafeteria and was stabbed by another prisoner. They don't know why."

My confusion turns to shock. My father is gone? Dead. He can't be dead. I hate him for what he did to my family, to Charlotte. Though I wanted him to pay for what he did, I never wanted him to die. He was my father, and part of me still loves him, for that reason alone. I even had the naïve hope that once he served his time, he would come back a different person. Now he won't be coming back at all. A single tear tracks down my cheek and I swipe it away. Why can't I get control of my emotions?

"I'm on my way back to the city, Mom. I will call Ashley to cancel the board meeting and come straight to you." My mom still loves my father. She may have divorced him after he kidnapped Charlotte, but she still loves him. She doesn't need to be alone right now.

"No. You go to the board meeting and tell them what's happened. Charles may not have been a part of the company any longer but this will reignite the media. You've worked so hard to keep the company going, don't let this tear it down. Take care of the business first and then come here." Mom's sobs are all but gone, her resolve strong.

"Are you sure, Mom? I can come there and handle the work stuff later?"

"I'm sure, Raeford. I loved your father, but I haven't forgotten why he was in that god-awful place to begin with. You do what you have to do, and this afternoon you and Daniel can come over here. I need to call Marie and see if she can get a flight. Since she was coming later in the week for the wedding maybe she can change her ticket." Mom sounds like her normal self again. Feisty.

"Okay. I'll head on to the office then. I need to get a press release out." I'm not looking forward to dealing with the media all over again. "I'll be over as soon as I can. Have you told Daniel?"

"No, will you call him? I need to get in touch with Marie and then call the funeral home. I want to make sure any service we decide to have is immediate family only." Mom is right about that. We don't need a media circus around a funeral.

"I'll tell Daniel. And I agree on the funeral. Just us. With all that happened, it's for the best." There are people who will want to comfort my mother, but those close to her will do it outside of a formal setting. "Hang in there, Mom. I love you."

"I love you too, son. I'll see you later today. Bye." Mom ends the call and I am left in silence as I drive.

My father is dead. My chest tightens as I remember the good times with him. Flashes of the days of me following him around as a child, mimicking his every move, plague me. He always made sure I knew that my destiny was to follow in his footsteps at Alvero & Alvero, even when I was a small child. My thoughts turn to the more recent events and I become angry again. How could a man I loved and respected so much do the things to me he did? He did all he could to keep me from the woman I love and even tried to take my child away from me. How can I still love him after that? And how am I supposed to feel now that he is gone? There are no answers as I continue toward the city.

I shake my head in an effort to clear my thoughts. It doesn't work but it does remind me that I need to call Daniel. I quickly press his number on my dash screen, not knowing if he will answer.

Daniel came in as a corporate attorney with the company after I took over. It turns out the reason he never worked for it before was all due to our father. With him out of the picture in the company, Daniel was happy to come on board, and I was thrilled to have him. His law firm hated to lose him but I was relieved knowing that I now had a great legal advisor on our team.

After a few rings, he finally picks up.

"How did it go at the house?" Daniel asks without even saying hello. I had forgotten about my morning after the call from Mom.

"Great. I put in an offer. That's not why I am calling though." I pause to gather myself. "Mom called. Dad was killed in the jail cafeteria, stabbed by another prisoner."

"Well. Guess that fucker got what he deserved." Venom

laces Daniel's voice. "He definitely won't hurt anyone else now."

I am taken aback by Daniel's response. Dad's harsh and demeaning attitude toward Daniel meant they were never close, but I expected him to be at least a little upset about his death. I didn't think his hatred for our father went this deep.

"He's still our father, Daniel. Don't you feel anything?"

"Relief. I feel relief. Now I don't have to worry about him getting out and trying to hurt Mom. I loved him because he was my father, but I hated him more than I loved him. He made my life hell long before you knew it." There is no anguish in Daniel's words. Maybe I shouldn't be as upset as I am. Especially after what Dad did to my family. Hearing Daniel makes me even more confused about my feelings.

"You're right. I know. I'm just in shock, I think. I'm headed to the office for the board meeting. Will you come in with me to inform them of what has happened? We need a plan to control the publicity."

"Of course. I'll be there." Daniel pauses as if thinking. "Raef, don't think you shouldn't be sad. You were very close to Dad for a long time." Daniel ends the call with no further words and I am again left in silence.

As I near the office, I realize I haven't told Gemma. I almost hate to make the call because I know she will share the same feelings as Daniel. Her reaction is sure to make me feel as guilty as Daniel's did. How can I grieve over an evil man? Sighing, I click on Gemma's number. She needs to know. She answers after only one ring.

"Hey, Raef." Gemma's sweet voice soothes me, even though I was worried about calling her.

"Hey, beautiful." Gemma giggles as usual, but I keep going. "I have some news to tell you. It's quite disturbing."

I take a deep breath.

"What is it, Raef?" I hear concern in Gemma's voice.

"My father was murdered in jail this morning." Gemma's gasp echoes throughout my car.

"Oh no, Raef! I am so sorry!" She's truly upset by the news. Such a different reaction than I expected. I even think I hear her crying softly. Gemma has such a big heart. This man kidnapped our child and tried to keep us apart, yet she is upset over his death. How did I get so lucky?

"It's a shock for sure." I tell Gemma what little details I know about what happened. I end with, "I really don't know how to feel about it."

"You feel heartbroken. That's how you feel. No matter what he did, he was your dad. Losing your dad is not easy no matter the circumstances. You're entitled to mourn him." My heart swells as Gemma speaks. She understands me so well.

We talk for a few more minutes until I pull into the parking garage at the office. I feel much more at ease than I did before I talked to Gemma. My heart doesn't hurt as much. I actually think I can get through this meeting and keep my composure.

Chapter 5

GEMMA

MY EMOTIONS ARE ALL OVER the place when I end the call with Raef. I hated his father for what he did to Charlotte, but my heart breaks for Raef. I feel guilty that a part of me is relieved that I never have to worry about Charles Alvero again. How can I face Raef while having these feelings about the death of his father? I need to talk to someone who will listen and not judge me. I need to talk to Kathleen. With Charley at the sitter, I decide to make a trip to the farm.

While I drive, I think about Raef. He sounded so broken on the phone. How could he not be? The man he idolized until recently has been torn from his life not once, but twice. This last time being final. And what of Ruth Alvero? She seems to be such a strong woman but could this break her? She loved her husband enough to put up with so much out of him over the years. Only when he kidnapped Charley did she end their marriage. I can't imagine what she must be feeling.

This is another one of those times I wish my mom was still here to talk to. But, she's not. Kathleen is. I turn down the drive to Jack and Kathleen's house and begin to feel slightly better. Kathleen will be able to help me through this. As much as I try not to burden her with my problems, I find myself thinking of her as a surrogate mother more and more. Today is no different. I need a mom and Kathleen will fill that void for me.

I notice Max's truck parked close to the barn. It's odd for him to be visiting his parents during the work day. Maybe Jack needed help with something. I hope I'm not interrupting family time with them. Before I can get out of the car, the door to the house flies open. Kathleen runs toward me.

"Hey, Kathleen." I meet her at the front of my car. She immediately grabs me into a hug.

"Oh, Gemma. I'm so sorry!" Kathleen holds me tightly. "It's all over the news about Raef's father."

"Really?" I'm surprised it has been picked up so quickly. "The family just found out. How did the press get a hold of the news so fast?" I pull away from Kathleen. Raef has to be even more upset now. He has worked so hard to get the media off the story about Charley's kidnapping and now this.

"I don't know. It's just a mess." Kathleen pulls me through the door of the house. Jack and Max both approach me as soon as we are inside.

"So sorry, baby girl." Jack hugs me. I enjoy the comfort of his embrace.

"Bastard got what he deserved," Max bites out.

"Max Greenwood!" Kathleen berates. "Watch your mouth. No one deserves to be murdered."

Max's scowl becomes more pronounced. He turns and disappears to the kitchen. Kathleen guides me to a chair in the living room where we all sit. All except Max. I am thankful for the moment alone with Jack and Kathleen.

"How is Raef?" Kathleen asks.

"Upset and feeling guilty because of it. He's handling

business this morning but headed to his mom's after lunch."

"He should feel guilty." Max stomps back into the room with a bottle of water in his hand. "He shouldn't be sad over that man,"

"Max." The one word from Jack stops Max. "Keep your thoughts to yourself, son." Max drops into a chair, but doesn't say anymore.

"Raef isn't the only one feeling guilty." I tuck my head as I speak. "I am, too. I am because I'm glad he's gone." A tear trails down my cheek.

"Oh, sweetheart!" Kathleen sits beside me and embraces me. "Don't feel guilty about that. All you know of the man has been the hurt he caused your family."

"She's right. It's different for you. You have no good memories of the man like Raef does." Jack reaches over and pats my hand. "You're entitled to be relieved, just as Raef is entitled to grieve."

I know they are both right, but I am still ashamed of how I feel. Kathleen holds me while I cry. Jack sits in silence, supporting from a distance. Their words do make me feel better. My main worry now is how to comfort Raef's grief. He needs me to be a better woman than I feel right now.

As if reading my mind, Kathleen breaks the silence. "You'll know how to be there for Raef when you see him." Kathleen kisses me on the cheek before standing. "I need to check on lunch. I hope you'll stay a little longer and eat with us." I nod to let her know I will.

Jack also stands. He pauses in front of me as if in deep thought. After a few moments, he takes my hand in his. "Be there for your young man. Support him when he needs you. Doing that doesn't mean you have forgotten what Charles Alvero did to you. It just shows you love your mate." He places a kiss on my hand. "I need to get back to the barn. Give Raef my condolences."

Jack is a quiet man so when he speaks it is always of substance. I think about what he says and realize he is right. I can be there for Raef. I can love him and comfort him without thinking of my feelings. That's what relationships are about, being there for each other. I suddenly feel much better than when I got here.

"Gem." I flinch, not realizing Max is still in the room. "Will you walk out on the porch with me?" Max asks. It seems like a strange request but I nod and head outside.

I walk to the end of the porch and look across the beautiful expanse of the farm. This view of the open land extending to the vast tree line has always calmed me. Leaning against a pole, my mind wanders to Raef. I am deep in my thoughts when hands rest upon my shoulders. I turn to see Max only inches from me.

"Gemma." Max's voice is soft and quiet. His brow is furrowed as if he is troubled. "I need to say some things to you. I need you to hear me out."

"Okay." I have no idea what Max could be about to tell me, but I feel like I may not like it.

Max turns away from me. He takes a deep breath and looks toward the ceiling before turning back to me. The expression on his face is unreadable. He takes my hands in his.

"Gemma. Don't marry Raef." My mouth drops open. "I can take care of you and Charley." Take care of us? Why would we need him to take care of us? We have Raef. I step away from Max so he is no longer touching me.

"What are you talking about, Max? I love Raef. Why wouldn't I marry him?"

"You don't need all this drama that follows the Alvero family. You and Charley deserve a calm life. I can give that to you." Max's shoulders are tight with tension. The look in his eyes is almost desperate.

"Max, where is this coming from?" I still don't understand what he is saying.

"I love you, Gemma. I have loved you since we were kids. Don't marry Raef. Marry me," Max pleads, anguish on his face. He reaches for me again.

I step further away, out of his reach. Why is he telling me this now? I shake my head and continue to walk backwards. I don't want to have this conversation with Max. Even though we were married, we never felt romantically about each other. He just wanted to take care of me after my parents died. That's all it ever was.

"No, Max. Just no. I am marrying Raef. I love him. You don't love me like that. We are just friends. You know I love you as a friend." I have worked my way to the steps. "I have to go." I start down the stairs, grateful that I left my keys in the car. Max's footsteps echo across the porch.

"Wait! Gemma, I do love you! Don't go!"

Max has almost reached me when I run into the solid wall of Jack Greenwood. Jack backs me away from him. He has a scowl on his face much like the one I see on Max all the time.

"Son. Stop. Let her go." Jack looks back to me. "Go to your young man and forget what just happened here. I'll handle Max." He tilts his head toward my car.

I run the last few steps to my car in a rush to leave. Jack berates Max. "She isn't yours, son. She loves another man. Let her go." I quickly close my door. I can't bear to hear more. Max drops his head while his father continues. I am in total shock from Max's confession of love. I've never suspected he had feelings for me other than friendship.

I just thought my emotions were all over the place on the drive to the farm. That was nothing compared to them now on the drive back. I don't want to lose Max as a friend but if these feelings he shared are a problem, then our friendship may not be sustainable. I love Raef with my whole heart and I won't put us in a position for him to question that. I don't even know how to tell Raef about this with everything else that has happened today. This has been a horrible day.

Chapter 6

RAEF

I FINALLY PULL INTO THE APARTMENT complex around midnight. After such a long miserable day, I can't wait to get inside and see Gemma. I am exhausted, mentally and physically. I spent the afternoon running back and forth from Mom's house to the office. The media coverage of Dad's death has exploded like a firestorm. I tried to run damage control while being there for my family, but it has been difficult.

When I open the door to the apartment, the last thing I expect to see is Gemma asleep on the couch. I had told her earlier to go on to bed and not wait up for me. She looks so peaceful I hate to wake her. I can't help myself, though, I need to hold her. I sit on the couch for a few moments and watch her sleep. As I caress her cheek with my hand, her eyes flutter open.

"Hey." Gemma's sleepy voice makes me smile.

"Hey, yourself." I lean over and press my lips to hers. I meant for it to be a sweet wake-up kiss but I need her so much after today. The kiss quickly becomes heated. I finally pull away and smile down at her. "I missed you."

"I missed you, too. How are you? How's your mom?" My sweet Gemma, always thinking of everyone else.

"I'm okay, just tired. Mom's actually doing really well. Daniel stayed with her tonight and Marie will be in tomorrow." Gemma sits up on the couch and lays her head on my shoulder. We snuggle back into the couch and I sneak another kiss from her. "We have decided not to have a funeral. Mom's idea. He's going to be cremated."

"Are you okay with that? Don't you want to have a proper service for your dad?" Gemma asks me.

I move a stray hair from her face. "Actually, I am. I can't forget what he did to us, to Charlotte. It's better for all of us not to create a spectacle with a service. Plus, the press would be all over it. They have been camped outside Mom's house all day." It angers me that they won't leave my mother alone. They think if she steps outside her own home she should give them an interview. That's not happening.

"Oh, Raef. That's horrible."

"It is. Mom's going to go back to New York with Marie after the wedding just to get out of town for a while. Hopefully the story will fade quickly." I pull Gemma onto my lap. It's as if I can't get close enough to her tonight.

"Do we need to put off the wedding?" Gemma wrings her hands in concern.

"Absolutely not! My father is not going to mess this up for us. I am marrying you this Saturday." Gemma bites her lip and frowns. She is still concerned. I tilt her head to just the right angle to kiss her with enough love and passion to wipe the concern away. She will be my wife in a few days. Nothing is going to stop that.

"Okay," Gemma gasps as she pulls her lips from mine. I moan as she moves on my growing erection. That gets a giggle from my girl. She takes my hand and pulls me to a standing position.

"Where are you taking me, soon-to-be Mrs. Alvero?"

I tease as Gemma leads me down the hall. "Do you have more surprises planned for me?" I allude to last night. It seems like so long ago.

"I'm taking you to bed. You need to get some rest."

"Hmmm." I place kisses on the side of Gemma's neck. I want to forget the events of the day by being deep inside of her. "Not sure rest is what I need right now."

"Well, rest is what you're getting."

"Ugh," I groan. "You can't sit on my lap and kiss me like that, then expect me to want to rest."

"I believe you pulled me on your lap and *you* kissed *me*, Mr. Alvero. And I believe you need some rest." Gemma shuts our bedroom door and pulls out her pajamas. That's sure not what I want to see her in. I grab the pajamas away from her before she can do anything with them.

"If you want me to rest, you need to forgo these. Just you and me, skin to skin." I drop the pajamas on our dresser and proceed to take off my clothes. Gemma hesitates for only a moment before she follows and takes off her own.

I lay on the bed and watch as she finishes undressing. I am one lucky man. I pat the bed next to me and watch her crawl over the covers. I was hard before from just watching her undress. Her sexy little ass crawling across our bed has me almost in a state of pain. I grab her when she gets close and have her under me in a flash. She throws her hand over her mouth as she squeals then laughs.

"Laughing at me, babe?" I drag my kisses from her lips to her neck.

"Nope, laughing at me for squealing. It would be terrible if I woke Charley."

"That would be a bit of a problem." I trail my kisses back up to her lips. "I plan to lose myself in you right now. I need you, Gemma."

"Find your comfort with me, Raef." Gemma takes me

in her hand and guides me to her center. I ease inside her and when I am fully seated, I pause. I whisk Gemma's hair from her face.

"You feel so good, Gem. This is where I need to be. Deep inside of you." I kiss her softly but this time it quickly ignites with passion. Gemma's hands slide up and down my back, leaving chills in their wake. I rock inside of her, measured at first, before my pace quickens. Nothing in the world feels like being inside of her.

Decreasing my speed, I'm not ready for this to end. I prop myself on my elbows where I can look at Gemma. The passion on her face is almost my undoing. Her eyes are closed and her lips are parted as she pants with my thrusts. I keep up the lazy tempo while I watch my beautiful Gemma below me. Soon, I can't take it any longer and pick up my momentum again. I move within her furiously, closing in on the finish. Wanting Gemma to finish with me, I reach between us.

"Look at me, Gem. I want to see your eyes when you come." Gemma opens her eyes just as I circle my finger on her nub of nerves. She immediately goes over the edge. I drive myself into her as she clenches around me and shatter, calling her name. I hold myself over Gemma for a few moments, still deep inside her. I don't want to leave her but I know I am heavy. I slide out of her and she moans against me. Once we are both under the covers, I pull her tightly against my side.

"Wow, babe. That turned an atrocious day around." Our breaths are still heavy as we snuggle into each other.

"I agree. Horrible day with a great ending." Gemma wears a defeated frown. It's like she may have dealt with more than Dad's death today. Her entire demeanor just changed.

"Was your day bad because of what was going on with

my dad? Or did something else happen?" I roll to my side so I can look in her eyes.

"Now really isn't a good time to tell you this but I don't want to keep it from you." Gemma has me concerned. What else could have happened today?

"What is it, babe? What happened?"

"After I talked to you this morning, I went out to the farm. I wanted to talk to Kathleen. I hate to admit it, but I was feeling guilty about what I felt about your dad's death. I needed Kathleen's level head to get me straight." Gemma pauses.

"Is that all, babe? Are you worried I'll be upset with you? Trust me, I have some feelings that I probably shouldn't have also." I feel a bit of relief. She had me concerned something had happened.

"No. That's not all. Max was there. He said some things he shouldn't have said. Things that may mean we can't be friends with him any longer." A tear escapes from Gemma's eye. I quickly wipe it away. Anger builds in me. Why does this guy have to pull some stunt today of all days? The last things she needs is to deal with him and his problems.

"What did he say?" My tone sharp.

"He tried to convince me not to marry you. He said he loves me and wants me to marry him."

My heart squeezes and my chest tightens. Surely Gemma won't leave me for Max. He was there for her when I left her before. Have I proven myself enough to earn her trust back? We just made love. That has to mean something. My chest literally hurts as I try to find my voice. Do I want to ask what her response was?

"Oh. Wow." I hesitate as I look away from Gemma. "What did you say?"

Gemma turns my face back to hers. She gazes directly

into my eyes. "I told him I love you, Raef. And that I am going to marry you. Then I left."

I let out a huge breath of relief. I pull Gemma tightly against me and kiss her, over and over.

"Thank God! I can't lose you again." I continue to kiss her like my last breath depends on it.

"You won't lose me, Raef. I will choose you every time. Never doubt that." Gemma kisses me back as hard as I am kissing her.

Sorrow streaks down my cheeks. I went through the entire day without shedding a tear for my father. The thought of losing Gemma has brought my grief to the forefront. I can't seem to stop weeping. I sob against Gemma's lips but don't stop kissing her. She seems to understand I need this comfort.

My grief dries and I am hard all over again. I roll Gemma onto her back and slide back into her. I throw my head back in ecstasy as I drive in her. Gemma places kisses on my chest while I move at an extremely slow pace. There is nothing quick about this time. This time is about peace and comfort. Gemma is my peace. Being inside her is my comfort.

Chapter 7

GEMMA

Friday

THE TWINKLE LIGHTS ON THE porch work. The flowers are done. The cake has been delivered. Everything is in place. I can't believe it is almost here. I stand in the yard and look at the decorations. Kathleen has done a fabulous job of turning her porch into a magical place for us to exchange our vows. Even though it will be small, she made sure we will have a beautiful, special ceremony.

"Hey, girlie." Tiba flounces out the door. "What you doing standing out here staring at the porch?"

"It's just so pretty. I can't believe Raef and I will be married here tomorrow." I smile at the thought of beginning my life with the man of my dreams.

"You will be. Come on inside. Charley is ready to eat. Then we have to get back to town and meet everyone else. Party tonight."

I shake my head with laughter as Tiba dances on the porch. Tonight, Raef and I are going out for a few hours with our close friends and family. It will be our bachelor and bachelorette party all rolled into one. Neither of us wanted to be apart from the other, and this stressful week reinforced that.

Tiba and I walk inside and are met by a very exuberant Charley.

"Mommy, Auntie T! Come on! Let's eat!" Charley grabs our hands and pulls us both to the kitchen table. The smell of Kathleen's famous pot roast wafts through the air. Jack and Kathleen are already in their places. Once we settle into our chairs, Charley dives into her food. She has talked about the wedding all day long. I know as soon as she finishes her plate, it will be right back to it.

"How is your young man doing?" Jack asks.

"Actually, he's doing really well. He has moments where the grief grabs him but all in all, he is good."

"And his mom? How is she?" Jack has been upset with how the press has treated the family this week. The story of Charles Alvero's death has been the daily headline, with the media making issues of the family's choice to have no service.

"She's as well as can be expected. She loved her husband. She's going to have some rough moments. Good news is the press has moved out of her front yard." Once they realized there wasn't going to be an official service for Charles Alvero, the reporters moved on. Raef worked with some media contacts to try to turn the story to what happened inside the jail as opposed to the family's grief.

Charley has finished her meal and is now going on and on about the wedding. The rest of us enjoy our food and let her talk. When we finish, Tiba takes Charley to get her bath. She will spend the night here at the farm while Tiba and I meet the others in town.

I stay behind in the kitchen to help Kathleen clean up while Jack heads to the barn to feed the horses.

"So, Max told me Raef talked to him about what happened here the other day." Kathleen washes the dishes while I dry. My heart grips with fear that this issue with Max will change my relationship with Kathleen.

"I hope you understand why he did it. He really wants us to be able to be friendly with Max." I steal a glance at Kathleen. She stops washing and dries her hands. Her expression is solemn but calm.

"I totally understand and I don't blame Raef at all. Max was out of line. That boy holds things in for too long. All of this time and he never even shared his feelings with me or his father." Kathleen leans back against the counter. "As his mom, I hate to see him hurt, but he has to understand that you don't feel that way about him."

"I hate it too. I really do. But it doesn't change the way I feel. I love Raef."

Kathleen reaches for my hands. "I know you do, sweetie. Max will figure it out sooner or later. He'll realize you belong with Raef."

"I just don't want his feelings to keep us from spending time with you and Jack."

"Don't you ever worry about that. We're your family." Kathleen squeezes both hands. "Now, scoot so you and Tiba can get back to town. You have a party tonight."

"Thank you, Kathleen. Thanks for everything you've done for our wedding." I drop her hands and pull her into a hug before I leave the kitchen. Time to tell my little one goodnight and change clothes so we can head to town. I can't wait for Raef to see my outfit tonight. I decided it was time for another surprise.

Chapter 8

RAEF

WHEN I PARK IN THE bar's lot, Moss and Daniel pull in beside me. We could have ridden together, but I want to take Gemma to the new house later tonight. We tried to convince Marie to come with us, but she chose to stay with Mom. She's going to help Mom pack since they fly out after the wedding tomorrow. So, it will just be the three of us, Tiba, and my beautiful bride tonight.

I flinch at a knock on my car window. Moss and Daniel laugh at me. As I open the door, their laughter increases.

"What's got you so spaced out, little brother?" Daniel asks as I get out to the car. "Let me guess. Hmmm, could it be Gemma?"

Moss jumps into the action. "Yep, I think it may be Gemma. That girl sure has her hooks in you, doesn't she?"

"Shut up, both of you. I can't wait for the day the two of you fall in love with someone." That quietens them to muffled grunts and "not me." I enter the bar with a smile, until I spot Max at the bar. Even though I knew he possibly would show up, it dampens my spirits a bit. I had a chat with him a couple of days ago and made it clear that Gemma and I would be together. I told him that I appreciated all he did for her and Charlotte during those years I wasn't around, but I am here now. If we are all to remain friends, he's going to have to accept that. He apologized to me and claimed he will support my relationship with Gemma. I guess we are about to find out if he means it.

Moss and Daniel follow me to the bar and I sit next to Max. He doesn't look my way but I can tell by the way his shoulders tense he knows it's me. I order a beer before I turn to face Max.

"Hello, Max. Didn't realize you were coming tonight."

Max takes a long drink of his beer before looking my way. Defeat is in his eyes.

"Gemma invited me. Before I made an ass of myself."

"Well, I'm glad you came to celebrate with us." I hope this may bring us all together. "We plan to have a good time." I turn back toward Daniel and Moss. "This is my brother, Daniel, and my friend, Moss. Guys, this is Max, a friend of ours." Max's gaze flares a moment of shock when I say *ours*.

"Glad to meet you, man." Moss extends his hand across me to Max.

"Yes, good to meet you." Daniel waves from his spot down the bar. He then gives me a *what the hell* look. I just smile and take a drink of my beer.

We all chat as we drink. Even Max joins the conversation after a bit. I get a good amount of ragging from the guys for stealing glances at my watch every few minutes. They just don't understand how anxious I am to see my future wife.

Just as I look at my watch again, the door opens. I stop breathing. Gemma wears a short skirt, red tank top and red heels, something out of the norm for her. She looks amazing. My heart skips a beat. She spots me across the bar and our gazes lock. I am drawn to her and we meet in the middle of the room. There could be no one else here or a hundred people here but the only one I see is Gemma.

"Hey, beautiful. You look fantastic!" Gemma's eyes light up with my words.

"Do you really think so? I'm a little self-conscious. Tiba picked it out." She twists her hands. I reach out and take her hands in mine and pull her in for a kiss.

"I really think so." I kiss her again. Tiba walks by and grabs Gemma by the arm.

"Break it up. You two will have plenty of time for that tomorrow. Tonight, let's party!" Tiba pulls Gemma with her toward the bar. "Whoop, whoop, people! Let's get this party started!"

Gemma stops just before she reaches the others. She looks at Max and back to me. I wrap my arm around her and rest my hand on her hip, pulling her close enough to whisper in her ear. "It's okay. No problems." A quick kiss on the cheek and pat on the behind and we move on to join the others.

After the girls order their drinks, we find a table to fit all of us. Tiba carries the conversation and keeps the guys entertained. Gemma still acts a tad bit uncomfortable. She needs to talk to Max and clear the air. He may not be my favorite person, but his friendship means a lot to her. I can't blame him for loving Gemma, she's quite a woman. Plus, Jack and Kathleen have been very good to me since Gemma and I found each other again. I feel like it is important for us to be able to socialize with Max without feeling confrontational.

Max sits on one side of me and Gemma on the other. Deciding to try to fix the problem, I announce that I am headed to find the restroom. Before I go, I lean over and whisper to Gemma. "Move into my chair and talk to Max. You both need it." I walk away before she can respond but glance back. She is dumbfounded. I smile back and point to my chair. With a nod and a wink, I head on to the restroom.

I spend as much time as I can in the restroom without raising suspicion. I hope I have given Gemma enough time to talk to Max because I can't stay in here any longer.

Back at the table, Gemma is in my chair. She talks and Max nods as she speaks. I quietly slip into the chair Gemma vacated. She immediately turns to give me a kiss. I can't resist pulling her to me a little tighter. She whispers a quick "thank you" in my ear. I glance at Max and see he has joined back in the conversation going on at the table.

Our group enjoys ourselves for another hour or so. No one seems to notice that I stopped drinking early in the night. I am just biding my time before I can get Gemma out of here. It has been enjoyable to see Gemma relax and have a good time. Moss and Daniel have made jokes at my expense most of the night. I don't mind because it has made my girl laugh. The bar doesn't have a dance floor, but Tiba has danced with all the guys at the table. Moss seems interested in her, but she has blown him off at every turn. If I didn't know better, I would think Tiba has eyes for Max.

I glance at my watch and see it is almost eleven. I am more than ready to whisk my girl away. Gemma is in my lap so I lean closer. "Let's get out of here."

"Okay."

I'm a little shocked with her response but quite happy. I expected it to be harder to get her to leave. Gemma hops off my lap and I quickly stand with her. The rest of the table notices us and the conversation quietens.

"Where do you think you two are going?" Moss asks with a chuckle.

"We're out of here. I have a little surprise for my bride."

"Now, now." Tiba jokes. "None of that until after the wedding."

"That's right, little brother. Save it for the wedding night," Daniel joins in. Everyone at the table laughs and Gemma turns a cute shade of pink.

"Funny. You are a bunch of comedians tonight." Gemma giggles beside me. "Don't any of you stay out too late. We have a wedding tomorrow and all of you better be sobered up for it!" Gemma giggles again. Maybe I should be worried about how much *she* drank tonight.

A round of "don't worry," "we'll be there," and "be good" comes from the table. I shake my head at the raucous bunch as Gemma and I make our way toward the door. I can still hear our table of friends when we get out of the door.

"That's a crew in there isn't it, baby?" I lead Gemma to my car.

"They are something. I think everyone had fun." Gemma glides into the car. I lean over her to strap her in. It is a good excuse to steal another kiss from her.

"Did you have a good time?" I ask.

"I did! I don't get to unwind like that. It felt pretty good." Gemma looks at me suddenly like she just remembered something. "You said you had a surprise for me. What is it? Is it the same kind of surprise I gave you the other day?"

I can't help but chuckle at her question.

"Oh, you will get that kind of surprise sometime, but this surprise is something else."

"What is it?"

"You just have to be patient. You'll see soon enough." Gemma practically bounces in her seat. I chuckle again. The alcohol tonight has her much more carefree than usual.

"But I want to know now!"

"You sound like Charlotte," I tease. "Be patient, my dear. You will find out soon enough."

"Okay. I'll be good." My slightly inebriated bride giggles again. I love that sound. I love to make her happy.

We drive the rest of the way to the house without talking. Instead, we both sing along with the radio. Soon I turn into the driveway to the house.

"Where are we?" Gemma leans forward to look out the window. Porch lights glow at the end of the drive. I don't say anything as we pull up to the house.

"Whose house is this? Are we visiting someone tonight?" I motion for her to stay in her seat until I can get around to her side. I help her out and lead her a few steps closer to the house. She looks at me questioningly as we stop.

I came to the house earlier today so everything would be ready. I left the lights on so she could see everything. Inside I have things prepared so we can have a snack and then spend the night here. I nervously look at Gemma.

"This is your surprise, baby. This is our house. It's your wedding present from me. I hope you love it as much as I did when I first saw it. This is for you, for us, for our family." I stop rambling. Gemma stares at the house with her mouth agape. She slowly turns her head away from the house and looks at me.

"This is ours? We get to live here?" Tears build in her eyes.

"Yes, baby. We get to live here. Is that okay?" I am still anxious about doing this without her seeing it first. What if she hates it?

"It's more than okay! Look at that big front porch!" Gemma throws her arms around me. I wrap mine around her and hold her tightly. "Thank you, Raef. Thank you for this."

"I would give you and Charlotte the world if I could. We'll start with a house. Do you want to see the inside?"

Gemma jumps out of my arms, grabs my hand, and pulls me to the porch. "Yes! Yes! I can't wait to see it!" I hand her the key when we reach the door.

"Do the honors, Gem. Open the door to your new house." She takes the key and unlocks the door. Before she opens it, she turns back to me.

"*Our* house, Raef. Our house for our family." Gemma steps inside and gasps. I immediately worry she doesn't like it.

"What is it?" My worry increases when I see her hand over her mouth. She turns to me and wraps her arms around me again.

"I love it, Raef. It's beautiful!"

I let out a breath. She likes it so far. That's a very good thing. I take her hand and lead her throughout the downstairs. There is no furniture so our footsteps echo as we go. We take time in each area, with Gemma reverently touching each surface, from the mantle to the kitchen counter. She still has a look of amazement on her face. I lead her back to the grand staircase in the front of the house.

"Let's go upstairs so you can see the bedrooms." I kiss her hand.

"I'm so overwhelmed with this floor that I can't even imagine the upper floor!"

"There are three bedrooms and the master up there. We can let Charlotte pick her room and then I'll paint it pink." I smile when I think of my little girl running around this house. She will be so excited with her new room and with the huge yard.

Once upstairs, we walk through the bedrooms and bathrooms. Gemma points out the one she thinks Charlotte will choose. I agree with her but then again, who knows with a four-year-old little girl. She continually surprises me.

The door to the master bedroom is closed. I have another surprise for Gemma inside. Before I turn the knob, I look at Gemma.

"This is our bedroom, baby. This is our sanctuary from the outside world." Gemma smiles and nods but doesn't speak.

When I open the door, I step back to let Gemma enter first. She gasps again as she peers around the room. A new king-sized bed is the majestic focal point in the room. Matching furniture and complementary fabrics complete the room. Rose petals adorn the top of a solid white comforter. I listened to the interior designer and put many pillows at the top of the bed. I still don't understand the need for all the frou-frou pillows but the designer said Gemma would love it. By the look on Gem's face, she was right.

"So, what do you think?" I wrap my arms around Gemma's waist from behind and nibble on her neck while she continues to look around the room.

"It's beautiful! And so big! And it has furniture!" Gemma twists around in my arms. "Oh, Raef! I absolutely love everything. This is the best surprise ever!" Gemma kisses me. I deepen the kiss as I pull her tightly to me.

"I'm glad you like it. I hope the furniture is okay. I wanted you to have a finished bedroom when you first came here, but you get to pick out the rest of the house." Gemma's smile lights up her entire face.

"I love the furniture. And the bedding is gorgeous!"

"Great!" I kiss Gemma quickly. Before I let myself get out of control, I have one more thing for her to see. I lead Gemma through the room to the master bath. "This is your place to relax." Gemma squeals when she walks into the room. I can't help but chuckle when I see the expression on her face.

"Oh my goodness! This bathroom is perfect!" Before I know it, she has climbed inside the huge jetted tub. I sit on the side as she gushes on and on about the room. I point out the glass shower and the double sinks. I leave her in the tub and open one of the closet doors. Gemma squeals again and jumps up.

"This one is your closet, baby."

Suddenly, Gemma is inside the closet. "Raef! This is as big as my bedroom in the apartment!" Gemma runs her hands over the built-ins.

"It is big. There's another closet over there." I point to the other door in the bathroom. "It will be mine. It's only slightly smaller than this one."

"I can't believe this is really ours." Gemma's voice drops almost to a whisper. "I won't ever be able to thank you enough for this, Raef."

"You don't have to thank me, baby. This is our home." I pull Gemma to me. I gently place my lips on hers and kiss her softly. I feel Gem's tongue tentatively skim across my lip. I moan and deepen the kiss. My tongue tangles with hers. My hand slips under her shirt to find her skin. This time she moans against me. Breathless, I pull back and lead Gemma back to the bedroom.

"Wait here. I have to get something." I leave Gemma on the edge of the bed and go back into the bathroom. I have an ice chest with champagne and cheese hidden in my closet. I grab it and the basket that holds a tray, glasses, and crackers.

"I brought us a little snack."

Gemma has crawled to the center of the bed and sits with her legs crossed. I pass her the tray with the cheese and crackers arranged on top and two champagne glasses.

"I thought a little bubbly was in order, to celebrate our new home." I work to open the champagne bottle and get the usual pop when I succeed. Gemma holds out the glasses for me to pour. I place the bottle on the bedside table and take a glass from her.

"To our home." I toast. Gemma clinks her glass to mine.

"To our home." We both take a sip of the champagne.

Gemma and I gaze into each other's eyes for a long moment. I break the connection to get a cracker and cheese to feed Gemma. We both laugh when cracker crumbs fall on the bed. As we take turns feeding each other, I am amazed at the intimacy. When we finish the glass of champagne, I move everything from the bed to the table.

"Now we sleep." I pull back the covers for us. Gemma's expression is so cute I can hardly contain a smile.

"Sleep?" she asks. "I thought . . . well, I thought . . ." Gemma turns a perfect shade of pink.

"I know what you thought, but it's the night before our wedding. Tonight, we sleep because tomorrow night, there will be no sleep at all." I pull Gemma close to me, tuck us in and kiss her gently.

"Promises, promises, Mr. Alvero." Gemma giggles as she snuggles into my side. "I'll hold you to those promises tomorrow night."

"You can rest assured, soon-to-be Mrs. Alvero, those promises will be fulfilled. Now sleep. We've got a big day tomorrow." I kiss her one more time.

We snuggle in comfortable silence, and soon I feel Gemma's breaths even out. I glance to confirm that she is asleep. In a few short hours, she becomes my wife. I drift off to sleep with visions of my little family filling this house with love and laughter.

Chapter 9

GEMMA

Wedding Day

TIBA FINISHES MY HAIR AND hands me a mirror. I smile at my reflection. Curls cascade down my back. My makeup is more than I usually wear, but is still soft and natural. Tiba has done a wonderful job.

"Wow, Tiba!" I say as I hand her the mirror. "I've never looked so stunning."

"Girlie, you look beautiful all the time, but today? Today you look magnificent."

Before I can respond, the door opens and Kathleen walks in with Charley. Their chatter stops when they see me. Charley runs to me and jumps into my lap.

"You look pretty, Mommy!"

"You look so beautiful, Gemma!" Kathleen chimes in. My cheeks warm from the attention.

"Thank you both! Tiba did a great job on my hair and makeup." I give Charley a quick hug and kiss before I move her from my lap. "I just need to put on my dress."

Tiba brings the dress from the closet and unzips the bag. My stomach flutters like it did the first time I laid eyes on this dress.

I run my hand across the lace. I wish my mom was here. The thought hits me hard. All during the wedding planning, I have tried to keep my sadness at bay. Not having either of my parents to share this day with me could push me into a state of depression if I let it. I am determined for that not to happen. They are both here with me, just not in bodily form. I smile at the thought. They would want me to enjoy every moment of today, and that is exactly what I plan to do.

"Who wants to help me into this?" I ask with a smile.

"Me, Mommy! Me!" Charley jumps up and down. We all laugh at her exuberance.

"Of course you can help, little one." Kathleen takes the dress and lowers it for me to step into. "You hold this other side so your mommy can climb in." Charley eagerly, yet gently, takes hold of her side of the fabric.

"Don't fall, Mommy!"

I chuckle as I step into the dress. Kathleen and Charley raise it until Charley can't reach any higher. Tiba takes over for her and when the garment is fully on my body, she steps aside so Kathleen can zip the back.

"Take your mommy over to the mirror, Charley." Kathleen prompts when she has me zipped up. I glance back. Tears well in her eyes. Charley grabs my hand and pulls me toward the mirror.

"Come on, Mommy! Come see how pretty you look!" I follow Charley's lead across the room and stop in front of the mirror. I slowly raise my gaze to see my reflection. My breath stills. I had forgotten how much I love this dress. I can't seem to pull my gaze away.

"Tiba, would you mind taking Charley to her room and get her dressed? Your dress is in there also." I hear responses, but I don't hear the words. I am too focused on my reflection, wondering what Raef will think when he sees me.

Kathleen's reflection joins mine in the mirror as she walks up behind me and gently reaches to hold my arms. Her smile makes me smile.

"You look so beautiful, Gemma," Kathleen whispers to me. "Your parents would be so proud of you."

"Thank you. That means so much to me."

"I wanted a few minutes alone with you." Kathleen turns me away from the mirror and leads me over to the dresser where I see my bouquet. It wasn't there earlier; Kathleen must have brought it when she came in. She picks up the bouquet and holds it in front of me.

"So, you are supposed to have something old, something new, something borrowed, and something blue. Your dress is new, that's covered. I spent a lot of time thinking about the other three things and this is what I've come up with." Kathleen pauses for a moment and hands the bouquet to me. "If you look at the stem of your bouquet, I've added a lace handkerchief. This was your mom's and she carried it at her wedding. I still remember that day like it was yesterday. I hope you don't mind that I went through a box of your parents' things from the storage building here at the farm. I wanted you to have something that was hers."

I look at the handkerchief, fingering the delicate lace. It is perfect. A piece of my mom on my special day.

"I love it, Kathleen. Thank you for this." I reach to embrace her but she stops me.

"Wait just a minute. Now for the blue, look in the flowers." Kathleen tilts the bouquet where I can see a small blue frame nestled in the midst of the flowers. Inside the frame is a picture of my father smiling back at me. My vision blurs with tears. "Now he can escort you too," Kathleen says quietly.

Emotions overtake me and I grab Kathleen. As I pull

her into the tightest hug I can give her, tears escape the confines of my eyes. Kathleen hugs me back just as tightly before she pulls away and grabs a tissue to dab the tears away from my face.

"Tiba will kill me if she finds out I made you mess up your makeup."

I can't help but smile. "Oh, Kathleen. This is so, so incredible. Thank you so much. You have no idea what this means to me!" The thought of having my father and mother with me, even if only in these mementos, means so much. The fact that Kathleen went to the trouble to do this for me means even more.

"I know how thrilled they would be that you found your happy ever after. You were their world. We have one thing left." Kathleen turns to the jewelry box on the dresser and retrieves something. She opens my hand and places in it a pair of beautiful diamond earrings. "These are the earrings Jack gave me for our most recent anniversary. I would love for you to wear them as a symbol of what you mean to the two of us. They can be your something borrowed."

I close my hand around the earrings and again have tears in my eyes. Kathleen notices and grabs the tissue, dabbing before they escape. I laugh and Kathleen does too.

"I would love to wear your earrings." I hug her again. "Thank you and Jack for everything you have done for me and for the wedding."

Kathleen takes the earrings and puts them in my ears. She then holds me at arm's length and turns me around in circles. After two times, with us both laughing, she stops.

"You look gorgeous." Kathleen kisses me on the cheek, glances at her watch and walks toward the door. "I am going to check on Tiba and Charley. I'll send Jack in. It's almost time."

My heart seems to skip a beat. It's almost time to marry Raef. I can hardly believe the moment is upon us. I think back over the last few months. I never imagined I could be this happy. I never imagined Raef would be back in my life. I certainly never imagined he would want me as his wife. I take a deep breath to stop the tears that threaten again. Like Kathleen said, Tiba will kill me if I mess up this makeup.

Just as I pull myself back together, there is a soft knock on the door. With one last look at my beautiful bouquet, I say, "Come in." Jack eases through the door, looking handsome in his suit and cowboy hat.

"Hey, sweetheart. You look beautiful." Jack hugs me.

"Thank you. You look pretty good yourself."

"Do you mind the hat? If you want me to take it off for the ceremony, I will." Jack looks a bit uncomfortable.

"Oh, Jack. There is no way I would make you take off your hat. It's a part of you and I want you just as you are." I hold out my bouquet where he can see it. "Did you know about this?"

"I did. Kathleen spent a lot of time to get it just right. She was a bit obsessive with it." He chuckles and I follow with a chuckle of my own. When Kathleen gets focused on something, she does become quite fanatical until she gets it exactly the way she wants it.

"Well, it's amazing. I have missed Mom and Dad more than usual lately, so this was just what I needed."

"They would have been so proud of you. You can be sure they are looking down today beaming with joy and pride." I smile at Jack's words.

"I think you're right. I think they are smiling down on us today."

There is another knock on the door. Jack and I answer, "Come in," at the same time. We both laugh as Kathleen comes in.

"Tiba and Charley are dressed. Everyone is here and Moss is outside ready to go. Oh, and your fine young man looks quite handsome out there waiting on you. I think it's time." Kathleen pulls me in for a hug and points to the door.

In the hall, I find Tiba and my beautiful daughter. They have on their pink dresses and Charley holds a little basket full of pink rose petals. She is adorable in her dress. Kathleen embraces each of us before she heads back outside. The four of us walk to the back door of the house. We will move from the side of the house around to the front porch where the ceremony will be performed.

We stop at the corner of the house, just outside the view of the guests. It is early evening and the sun is setting on the expanse of the farm. The weather couldn't be more perfect since it is a mild Louisiana night.

I can hear music playing softly. Raef and I chose to depart from traditional wedding music and go with something mainstream that we both liked. I hear the strains of *A Little More* by Skillet, our cue to begin. Tiba grins and strolls around the corner. Jack has Charley's hand in his and quietly reminds her to walk slowly. She nods to him and he drops her hand, tapping her on the back gently to move her forward. My sweet girl, her wired energy wound tight, disappears around the corner.

Jack and I step to the edge of the house. He takes my hand and places it in the crook of his bent arm. My heart races with excitement. Jack places his other hand over mine and looks down at me.

"You ready for this?" he asks. I take a deep breath to calm myself before I smile.

"I'm so ready."

Jack pats my hand and leads me as we step around the

corner of the house. I try to take everything in as we stroll toward the porch steps.

Tiba has just made it to the porch and slowly climbs the steps. Charley is ahead of us, walking bit by bit like she was told. She concentrates as she drops just the right amount of rose petals with each step. Our guests stand on the other side of the sidewalk so they can watch us as we enter. We didn't invite many people but all that we invited came. My attention turns to the porch as we near it. Pink and white flowers adorn the railing along with the little white twinkle lights. When we reach the sidewalk, we turn toward the porch.

In front of us at the top of the porch stairs, Moss waits in the center. Tiba stands just to his right. I don't see Charley so I look to Moss's left. She stands, grinning, in front of her father. The sight of Raef takes my breath away. I stall mid-step. He is dressed in a custom-made black suit and looks so handsome.

Jack looks down to see why I have stopped. When he realizes why, he laughs. I smile, but my eyes never leave Raef. Jack and I move forward again and Raef descends to the bottom of the steps. Our eyes are locked on each other.

Jack and I stop at the base of the steps, just in front of where Raef now stands. Raef's eyes glisten. My own tears threaten to spill over. Jack pats my hand again and removes it from his arm. He gathers me into a hug.

"Be happy, Gemma. Kathleen and I love you." Jack pulls back, takes my right hand and places it in Raef's hand. He clasps our hands between both of his. "Take care of her, Raef."

"I will, sir. Always." Raef answers with conviction.

Jack retreats to stand with Kathleen. Raef places a single kiss on the back of my hand. "You look stunning!" His gaze doesn't leave mine. He moves beside me to climb the steps together.

"Let's get married," Raef whispers in my ear. I nod quickly and we both chuckle as we reach the top where our wedding party waits.

Raef and I stop in front of Moss. I hadn't noticed Daniel earlier. He stands to Moss's left as Raef's best man. He smiles and nods to us. Charley runs over and gives me a hug.

"You gonna' marry my daddy now, Mommy?" Charley whispers loudly. Everyone laughs.

"Yes, baby girl. Yes, I am. Go stand with Auntie T." Tiba reaches for Charley's hand as I ease her that direction.

Moss clears his voice and begins.

"We are gathered here today to witness a celebration of the love between Raef and Gemma."

I take a deep breath and let it out with a smile. I am about to marry Raef. This day is perfect.

Chapter 10

RAEF

THIS IS REALLY HAPPENING. I am about to marry Gemma. She is devastatingly beautiful in her dress. I choked back the tears when I saw her. Of course, I nearly broke down when Charlotte hugged Gemma. Now we stand here in front of our closest friends and family.

"We are gathered here today to witness a celebration of the love between Raef and Gemma," Moss begins. "These two have not had the traditional path to marriage but now that they have found each other again, they have chosen to pledge their lives to each other. Raef and Gemma have written their own vows, so I will let them say them now."

Gemma hands her bouquet to Tiba. I take both of her hands in mine as we face each other. I didn't actually *write* my vows; I plan to just speak from my heart. The emotions of this moment almost overwhelm me. I take a deep breath and look up from our joined hands into Gemma's eyes. The warmth in her gaze suddenly grounds me. God, I love this woman.

"Gemma, I couldn't believe my good fortune when you came back into my life. And not just you, but the gift you brought with you—our daughter. You and Charlotte are the two most important people in my life now. I love you with all my heart. I will spend the rest of my life showing you just how much. I will spend the rest of my life loving you, protecting you, caring for you, providing for you, spoiling you. You make me a better man. You make me the kind of man I want to be. I will be the best husband you can imagine because you make me want to be the best. I will be by your side until death pulls us apart. That will be the only thing that can ever tear me away from you. I love you, Gemma. I love you more than you can ever imagine. I am so happy you are going to be my wife." Tears shine on Gemma's cheeks. I can't help myself and reach over to kiss her.

"Hey, now! Save that for the end," Moss berates with a chuckle. I pull back as everyone laughs along with him.

Gemma grips my hands. She trembles and I can tell she wants to wring her hands in nervousness, but I won't let her go. I squeeze her hands gently to let her know it's okay to take her time. She closes her eyes and takes a deep breath. When she opens them, she gives me a huge smile and begins.

"Raef, I spent many months thinking I would never see you again. Months that I told myself I didn't love you anymore. When I saw you again, I knew I was wrong. There was no way I would ever not love you. You have been my heart since the day we met. I love you with every fiber of my being. I am so grateful that we get to spend our lives together. You and Charley are my everything. I will spend the rest of my life being the best wife and mother I can be. You, Raef Alvero, are my happily ever after. I give you my heart, my love and my life. Only death can come between us. And even then, you will be my forever love."

Emotion lodges in my throat. A tear escapes my eye. Gemma's words are so special to me. She is so special to me. We stare into each other's eyes, hands still joined. The rest of the world fades away. I want to pull Gemma to me and I start to do just that when Moss speaks.

"The love between these two is obvious. Now we will have the ring exchange." Moss takes the rings from Daniel and Tiba. He holds them in front of us. "These rings symbolize the love you share, today, and every day."

I take Gemma's ring while she takes mine. I lift her left hand and slide the ring on her finger.

"With this ring, I pledge my love and life to you. With this ring, I marry you. With this ring, we become one." I raise Gemma's hand to my lips and kiss it lingeringly.

Gemma squeezes my hand. I know I have to let her hand go, even though I don't want to. She takes my left hand in hers, places the ring on my finger and pushes into place.

"With this ring, I pledge my love and life to you. With this ring, I marry you. With this ring, we become one." Gemma takes my hand and kisses it like I did hers. Her lips against my skin send a jolt through me.

"Now . . ." Before Moss can continue, I interrupt him.

"Wait just a second. I have one more thing." Gemma's brow raises in confusion. She doesn't know what I have planned. I reach into my pocket and pull out a tiny ring. I drop to a knee and motion for Charlotte to come to me. I take her tiny hand in mine and place the little gold ring on her finger.

"Charlotte, I may have missed the first years of your life, but today I promise you that I will not miss any more. This ring I give you today is a symbol of my promise to always be here for you. You are my baby girl and I love you very much." She bounces on her toes and throws her little arms around my neck.

"I love you too, Daddy! I love you so much!" I hug her back just as tightly as she hugs me. The guests respond to the moment with "awe" and "how sweet". There are even a few sniffles from the crowd. I remove her arms from around my neck. The grin on her face warms my heart.

"Go stand back with Auntie T so I can finish marrying your mommy." Charlotte giggles and runs back over to Tiba.

I stand and take Gemma's hands back in mine. The love in her gaze overwhelms me. Her smile could light up the entire farm. I hope she can see how much I love her.

"I love you, Raef," Gemma whispers.

"I love you, too."

Moss reaches out and gives my shoulder a squeeze. It's his way of letting me know he approves. I give him a nod in appreciation of his support. He steps back to continue the ceremony.

"Do you, Gemma Warren, take this man to be your husband?" For just a moment, the fear she might say no slips in. Before it can linger, she quickly responds.

"I do."

"Do you, Raef Alvero, take this woman to be your wife?" Moss asks me.

"I most certainly do," I respond as I squeeze Gemma's hands tenderly.

"Now that we have exchanged the vows and the rings and have shared the love," Moss announces, "I pronounce you man and wife." Before he can continue, I pull Gemma to me, place my hands on her face and kiss her, hard. Moss chuckles. "And you may kiss your bride."

Everyone cheers and laughs as I continue to kiss Gemma. My hands snake around to her back and, without leaving her lips, I dip her low. When I lift her back up, we are breathless. We laugh together beaming at each other.

Moss clears his throat.

"Well, then. Now that we have that behind us, ladies

and gentlemen, I present to you Mr. and Mrs. Raef Alvero

Gemma takes her bouquet from Tiba. I hold her hand in mine and reach my other hand in Charlotte's direction. She runs over to take it. Gemma, Charlotte and I stand at the top of the porch while the guests clap and cheer. We take the steps and at the bottom everyone surrounds us with congratulations. This is us. Surrounded with family and friends. This is the beginning of forever for our little family.

Epilogue

MAX

TWINKLE LIGHTS, PINK FLOWERS, DANCING, laughter . . . It all was more than I could take. So here I am in the barn shoveling horse manure. I am trying to be happy for Gemma. I really am. She seems to love Raef and he is Charley's father. It's so hard though. I have loved Gemma as long as I can remember. Mom tells me that I just think I am in love. She says I have become used to being there for Gemma and Charley and do love them, but that I am not *in love*. I think Mom is crazy. I know how I feel and I know I love Gemma.

I hear something from the other end of the barn, so I step out of the stall. Tiba heads my way, looking down and tip-toeing the entire time. For some reason, the sight makes me chuckle. She looks up when she hears me.

"What's so funny, big guy?" Tiba asks with a smile. I make it easier on her and walk to her so she doesn't have to come any farther into the barn.

"Just the sight of you in your dress and heals walking in the barn."

"Well, the last thing I want is horse shit on my good shoes," she responds indignantly but with a smirk.

"Can't have horse shit on a princess, now can we?"

"I am so far from a princess and you know it. But I do love shoes and these are some fine heels." Tiba points to her feet. I look down and see she is right. They are some very sexy shoes. The kind of shoes that I would want a woman to wear when she has nothing else on. I have a flash of Tiba doing just that. Where did that thought come from?

"So enough about shoes. What tore you away from Moss and brought you out here?" Moss has been hanging all over Tiba since last night at the bar. The dude has gotten on my nerves with that. He will leave tomorrow and Tiba will still be here. She doesn't need to hook up with somebody that is about to leave. Why can't he just leave her alone?

"No one had to *tear me away* from Moss, silly man. I'm out here because Charley is looking for you. She wants to dance with you." Tiba reaches down to pull hay out of her shoe. My mind again imagines her with nothing on but those shoes.

What is wrong with me? This wedding must have short-circuited my brain.

"I've had enough happiness for one day. Plus, I've been shoveling horse shit as you put it. I probably smell bad by now." I don't want to disappoint Charley, but I don't want to go back out there either.

Tiba grabs my arms, leans into my chest, and her nose rubs my shirt as she smells me. She's smelling me! What the hell? Tiba grips me tighter and takes one last breath before backing away from me. Before I know what I'm doing, I have my hands on her waist and pull her a step closer to me. My heart beats faster and my head is fuzzy. Am I about to pass out? What a crazy thought. But something is definitely wrong.

"You smell pretty good to me, big guy." Tiba smirks as

she looks up with her big chocolate eyes. I never realized her eyes have flecks of gold. They are beautiful and I can't seem to tear my gaze away from them. I also can't seem to find my voice. I just stare back at her. "So why don't you go make your niece a very happy little girl and dance with her."

"You have beautiful eyes." I hear myself say to Tiba but it doesn't sound like my voice. How have I never noticed how beautiful she is? What is wrong with me? I feel like I can't breathe. My heart is about to jump out of my chest. Maybe I'm having a heart attack. That's it. I should ask Tiba to go get help. I can't get myself to say that though. "I really want to kiss you right now."

Tiba's brown eyes never leave mine and the gold flecks seem to dance. Her face is closer to mine as she stands on her toes and leans toward me.

"Then, why don't you?"

Before I can stop myself, I pull her flush to my body and dip my head to hers. When our lips meet, my entire body feels like it is on fire. My heart beats even faster. I can't seem to control myself and the kiss quickly spirals with passion. My tongue slips in and finds hers. She meets me every step of the way. I have never felt like this when I kissed someone. Her body fits mine perfectly and I press her even tighter into me. Her hands roam my chest and leave sparks in their wake. My hands are in the curls of her hair, holding her mouth to mine.

Tiba pulls back and I let her. I need to breathe. We both stare into each other's eyes as we catch our breath. I see desire in the depths of her dark eyes. She takes two steps back from me. I want to stop her but I don't. I watch as she smooths her dress with her hands and then attempts to straighten her hair. Her style is wild and curly, so I didn't do much damage to it. She has a smear of her lipstick and I reach out to wipe it away. She lets me, but then backs away again.

"Um, you need to come out and see Charley." Tiba turns and quickly steps through the hay to the door of the barn.

"Tiba, wait!" I call after her but she doesn't stop. I watch as she runs out the barn door.

I decide to go out and see Charley. I don't want to disappoint her and for some reason, I don't want to disappoint Tiba either. I look down and realize that I need a few more minutes before I go anywhere. That kiss left me hard and anxious. My mind goes back to the kiss, and I feel myself harden even more. Dammit!

I have to make myself think of something other than Tiba. I can't seem to tear my mind away from her. What the hell just happened here?

Playlist

"*Until I Wake Up*"-*Acoustic Version*
J.R. Richards

"*Love Walks In*"
Van Halen

"*Tangled Up in You*"
Staind

"*Forever*"
Papa Roach

"*Breathe*"
Through Fire

"*How Did You Love*"
Shinedown

"*A Little More*"
Skillet

Acknowledgments

FIRST AND FOREMOST, I WANT to thank my husband for supporting me in my dream of writing. His constant support and patience with my writing keeps me on track.

I also want to thank my children for their support. Although none of them want to actually read the books I write, they support me by sharing them with others. Our children are all adults and say that they don't want to know where their mom/step-mom comes up with certain *aspects* of the stories.

I want to thank two special ladies for a piece of their lives that they allowed me to use in this book. The idea of the picture in Gemma's bouquet was not mine. Many years ago, I coached a little girl named Kara Thompson in softball. Her dad, Kirby, loved her so very much and it showed in everything he did. Not too long after that time, Kara's dad was killed in a tragic accident. The relationship between this little girl and her father reminded me of the relationship I envisioned for Gemma and her dad. Recently Kara was married and had a picture of her father in her bouquet. Thank you so much to Kara and her mom, Dawn Hebert, for letting me use their idea for Gemma. It fit perfectly into the story.

A special thanks to The Killion Group, Inc. for their work on the cover, blurb, editing and formatting. These ladies do a phenomenal job and I don't know what I would do without them.

Last but certainly not least, thanks to you, my readers. Thank you for supporting my dream by purchasing my books. Thank you for the wonderful words you have shared with me after reading book 1 in the series. You make it possible to tell my stories. Without readers, writers' stories are written in silence. Thank you again for taking a chance on a new author.

Keep your eyes out for book 2. As you saw in the epilogue, Max and Tiba are going to be one hot couple!

About the Author

GROWING UP IN RURAL LOUISIANA, I dreamed of one day being a writer. Although it took many years to achieve that dream, life has been fulfilling along the way. Being a wife and a mother are the things I consider my biggest accomplishments. My family is number one in my eyes.

By day, I work in a public school finance. At night and on weekends, I become a writer. Outside of work and writing, I enjoy reading, photography, and traveling. I am obsessed with all things Disney and Thirty Seconds to Mars. In addition to my husband and son, my three favorite men are Mickey Mouse, Jared Leto and Shannon Leto.

I can't forget to mention my two babies, Beaux, our half-Yorkie, half-Labrador doggie, and Kat, our larger than normal cat. They complete our little family and have helped with the empty-nest since our children have become adults. They are very spoiled and have a hard time understanding why they can't be in my lap when I am writing.

Connect With
C. Kaye

Email:
authorckaye@gmail.com

Website:
http://authorckaye.wixsite.com/ckaye

Facebook:
https://www.facebook.com/authorckaye

Twitter:
https://twitter.com/authorckaye

Instagram:
https://www.instagram.com/authorc.kaye/

www.ingramcontent.com/pod-product-compliance
Lightning Source LLC
Chambersburg PA
CBHW020641130626
46552CB00003B/1341